The Mouse in the Stout

And Other Surprises

The Mouse in the Stout And Other Surprises

By

Ken Anderson

Illustrations

by

Teresa Anderson

iUniverse, Inc.
New York Bloomington

The Mouse in the Stout and Other Surprises
More Poems to Amuse and Bemuse

iUniverse books may be ordered through booksellers or by contacting:

iUniverse
1663 Liberty Drive
Bloomington, IN 47403
www.iuniverse.com
1-800-Authors (1-800-288-4677)

ISBN: 978-1-4401-9404-7 (pbk)
ISBN: 978-1-4401-9407-8 (cloth)
ISBN: 978-1-4401-9406-1 (ebk)

Printed in the United States of America

iUniverse rev. date: 9/9/2010

To my many friends who through their expressions of enjoyment upon reading my first book, *The Stifled Piper and Other Strange Characters*, encouraged me to keep writing and create this second book of poems; to Jean, Barb the Babe from Bickleton, Kelly, and Jamie T., who all provided inspiration for poems in this book; and especially to my wife Joyce, my daughter Kathy, my son Bob and my daughter-in-law Teresa who supported me in this endeavor.

Contents

Preface

Although distribution of my first book of poems, *The Stifled Piper and Other Strange Characters*, was somewhat limited, the responses from those who read it were quite positive. This feedback stroked my ego sufficiently for me to continue writing and produce this second book. Well, perhaps ego stroking isn't the only reason. I still seem to have this compulsion to see the ordinary events of life in an unconventional way and to set the results to rhyme.

In this book you will, for example, see the Grimm's Fairy Tales characters Sleeping Beauty and Prince Charming in a different light, compare the amorous quirks of the praying mantis with those of humans, and journey down Utah's Green River with the Anderson clan. You will attend an eye-opening class reunion, see the differing views of a husband's recent retirement as perceived by him and his wife, become familiar with a number of most interesting ladies and find a light side to many other more-or-less mundane occurrences.

Although my objective is generally to document a humorous aspect of the ordinary events one encounters, in a few cases I may have slipped up and strayed over the border into more serious territory. Hence, I choose to characterize this as a book of humorous and whimsical poems. After all, funny, like beauty, is often in the eye of the beholder. "Whimsical" seems to encompass all of the rather offbeat poems in this book, whatever their level of humor.

In any case, my objective is to amuse both myself and others, with the intent and hope that this book will lead its readers to view the events in their lives in a different, and slightly whacky, way. Enjoy!

Acknowledgments

Jean, Janet, Jim (Jamie T.) Denovan, Barb (The Babe from Bickleton) and her husband Ron, and Kelly (the rail splittin' wife) are friends who inspired some of the poems in this book and who have graciously consented for me to use their names. Regarding the poem, "The Daring of the Green, or Andersons Away and Awash," my nieces Kristi and Becky and Kristi's friend Darnell have also consented for me to use their names, the "Uncle Tom" is my younger brother, now deceased, and Dan and Sheila are a young couple I met only briefly and whose last names and home towns I never knew. The names given in the poem, "The Gang," are the nicknames of myself and of friends from my younger days, all but two of whom, "Cheesie" and "Clyde," are now deceased. Other than these individuals, and public figures such as Annette Funicello, Orville Redenbacher and Dale Chihuly, all characters in these writings are fictional, and any resemblance to actual persons, living or dead, is purely coincidental.

A special acknowledgment is owed to my daughter-in-law, Teresa, who created the illustrations for this book and who assisted in its formatting and in interacting with the publisher.

Sights to Behold

The Mouse in the Stout

(Inspired by a news story about someone who claimed to have found a foreign object in her beverage container.)

One evening, in need of refreshment,
I opened a bottle of stout
And, fetching a glass from the cupboard,
Proceeded to pour the brew out.
I stood there in anticipation,
Observing the foamy head swell,
Then noted, with some consternation,
A wee mouse emerging as well.

Now, watching the fur-covered creature
There, bobbing about in the head,
One glance was much more than sufficient
To tell that poor mousie was dead.
I know not if now he's in Heaven,
Or down in that alternate place,
But I can attest, from the look that I took,
He'd expired with a smile on his face.

Prince Charming, or A Grimm Life Ain't All that Bad

While doing research for one of my poems, I leafed through a copy of Grimm's Fairy Tales. I noted a recurring theme, which led to the following:

A lovely princess, 'neath a spell,
was deep immersed in sleep
Until Prince Charming, handsome guy,
came to her castle keep—
Bestowed a kiss to break the curse,
and Sleeping Beauty rouse,
They wed, and live quite happily
inside the prince's house.

Snow White, upon an apple choked,
into a slumber fell,
Until the touch of love's first kiss
would break the witch's spell;
A handsome prince arrived and kissed
her sweet lips, by-and-by,
Then took her to his palace home—
you guessed it, yep, same guy.

Fair Cinderella, put upon
by step-sisters and mom,

Was saddled with the work of drudge,
and then denied the prom,
Until a fairy's magic touch
aligned her with the prince;
The two of them connected, and
played "footsies" ever since.

Now, here's a lad who got around,
and clearly played the field,
He sampled all the fairy tales,
and took what they would yield;
So, now for him, well, life is good,
it's quite a lot of fun,
He's merrily ensconced in his
ménage à trois, plus one.

The House of the Troll

My son and daughter-in-law had their Tacoma cottage re-painted in bright colors, reminiscent of Scandinavia, which is troll country. That, combined with the small cairns they piled up along the front, somehow brought the following to mind. The place draws a good deal of attention and frequent "thumbs up" from passersby.

If ever you visit Tacoma
There's one place you may want to go
To round out the total experience—
It's known as The House of the Troll.

Surrounded by houses quite common
This dwelling fulfills a brave role,
Providing the area with color—
This place called The House of the Troll.

Bold colors from old Scandinavia—
Bright turquoise, barn red, dusty gold—
Were chosen to highlight this structure,
Adorning The House of the Troll.

And though the effect is quite striking,
There's yet a bit more to be told,
For, piled up, wee cairns ranked before it
Stand guard o'er The House of the Troll.

Yet, as you approach this strange structure
You need have no fear, bless your soul,
No peril is like to befall you
From those in The House of the Troll.

Kind Troll, gentle Trollette, abide here;
They're cast from a different mold
Than trolls who lurk under dark bridges,
These folk in The House of the Troll.

If lucky, you might be invited
To step in, if you'd be so bold,
To munch "Troll-House cookies" (delicious)
Fresh baked at The House of the Troll.

So have a great time in Tacoma.
If seeing the sights is your goal
Be sure to round out to completeness,
And visit The House of the Troll.

Then, as you recite your adventures,
Quite often your friends will be told,
"We saw the glass art of Chihuly*,
Oh, yes, and The House of the Troll."

*A world-renowned creator of art glass, whose products are displayed prominently at numerous Tacoma locations

Class Reunion

As years rolled by my wife and I
observed the decades pass,
Then heard of a reunion for
my spouse's college class,
She pondered it and then remarked,
"By gosh, that might be fun,
It's been so long since I have talked
to hardly anyone.

I'd dearly love to visit them
and stroll down mem'ry lane—
It would be great to look upon
their faces once again."
She added, "Well, we've got the time,
and surely have the dough,
There's nothing that is stopping us,
so, come on, Hon, let's go."

I had some reservations, though,
as memory is served,
I harkened back to days at school
and what I had observed—
Recalling lads she used to date,
although a few were duds
Her class was sprinkled lib'rally
with handsome, muscled studs.

With just a twinge of jealousy
at last I acquiesced,

My wife proceeded to prepare
to look her very best,
Then newly gowned and freshly coiffed,
and made up to the nines
We headed for the gathering
to capture olden times.

We entered the reception hall,
I slowly looked about,
I scanned the male participants,
and that relieved my doubts—
For these one-time Adonises,
now paunchy, semi-bald,
Were nowhere near the handsome studs
my mem'ry had recalled.

I felt a touch of pity at
how far they had declined,
Yet, scarce suppressed a snicker, for
the years had not been kind.
And so I giggled inwardly,
for I could clearly see
These aging ex-lotharios
were not a threat to me.

Back in our room as I disrobed
I slowly scanned my "bod,"
I stood before the mirror, and
I muttered, "Oh, my God,"
Then lost my smug and cocky smile,
for I could plainly see
Good Lord, she'd married one of them,
and that old fart was me.

The Daring of the Green, or Andersons Away and Awash

This poem addresses an adventure at a family gathering some years ago. Although somewhat exaggerated, this is the way it will live forever in the memories of the participants.

The mountains called Uinta stand,
their heads against the sky,
Observing many oddities
that go parading by;
But ranked among the strangest sights
that they have ever seen
Was when the clan of Anderson
went rafting down the Green.

'Twas in the spring of eighty-two,
and yet another year
Saw Andersons assembling
from places far and near.
Red Canyon Lodge had beckoned us
to leave our winter's lair
To stalk the wily rainbow trout
and breathe the mountain air.

The Andersons from Utah towns
were there—more than a few,
And, yes, the Oklahoma branch

was represented, too.
A couple down from Washington
decided to attend,
And, in addition to that group,
young Kristi brought a friend.

Now, after days of visiting
and taking in the view
The group began to search about
for something new to do.
They scratched their heads and pondered it—
at last somebody laughed,
"I know a great activity—
let's rent a rubber raft."

The others all applauded then—
they said, "Yes! Rent a boat!
'Twill be a new adventure, gang,
to have a river float."
Then someone said, "But, wait a bit—
let's have a show of hands
To see how many want to be
in this intrepid band."

So, hands went up from Andersons
who wished to take a part,
And Kristi's friend, Darnell, said, "Sure,
I'll join you at the start."
Two honeymooners we had met;
Dan, Sheila, his fair bride,
Said, "Gee, we'd love to go along
on your exciting ride."

The hands were counted carefully,
and when 'twas done we knew
For us to fit within the boat

we'd need not one, but two.
We went down to the rental place
to get a couple rafts,
Then split into a pair of crews
to occupy the crafts.

The fisher folk, with Uncle Tom,
took off in Number One,
And vowed to fill the boat with trout
before the day was done.
The group assigned to Number Two
assembled at its barge—
We drew our lots to set the tasks,
and Kris wound up in charge.

Soon Captain Kristi's doughty crew
was settled in its craft,
And each one had a job to do,
arranged from fore to aft.
Brave Sheila, forward, watched for rocks,
Ken sat in back to steer,
While Dan and Becky plied the oars
and Darnell served the beer.

We launched the boat below the dam
and headed for the goal,
Some seven rugged miles away—
a place called, "Little Hole."
At times adrift through placid pools
we made our tranquil way,
At other times we bounced about
in rapids, foam and spray.

At last the goal lay close at hand,
the journey nearly done,
Yet one more rapid lay ahead

awaiting to be run.
We heard the roar and gazed upon
a boiling, churning flood;
A sight most surely guaranteed
to chill a rafter's blood.

With heads erect we shot ahead
to dare the maelstrom's wrath,
But felt dismay as we observed
a boulder in our path.
Then Sheila cried out, loud and shrill,
"We're bound to strike, I fear;
So hold on tightly, everyone—
and, Darnell, SAVE THE BEER!"

Yet, stout of heart, we bent our backs
to tiller and to oar—
We swerved aside, brushed by the rock,
as through the gap we tore.
Hurrah! We knew we'd passed the test,
we'd carried off the palm—
We left the boiling flood behind
and moved into the calm.

Then glancing up we saw, at hand,
the banks of Little Hole;
We felt the thrill of victory
and coasted to our goal.
We pulled our raft up on the shore,
and gave a little cheer,
Then paused to rest our weary bones—
and Darnell had a beer!

Denovan's Legs

A friend of mine once dropped off some papers at the apartment of an employee on his way home from a jog, still dressed in his running gear. The employee's roommate teased him about his bare legs, which led to the following thoughts about her reactions.

They tell of a teacher in our local school
Who's clearly regarded as nobody's fool;
Why, only two objects can shatter her cool—
They're Jamie T. Denovan's legs.

Espying fair Jamie attired in a kilt
The lassie in question proceeded to wilt;
Her last conscious words were,
"Lord, look at the 'built'
Of Jamie T. Denovan's legs!"

She's thankful for Jamie's involvement in sports
Which dresses him down to his athletic shorts;
She waxes ecstatic, I've heard the reports,
O'er Jamie T. Denovan's legs.

Oh, what is evoking those maidenly sighs,
Those soft little murmurs, the stars in the eyes?

'Tis merely the thought of the calves and the thighs
On Jamie T. Denovan's legs.

She offers her prayer of ultimate greed,
"Oh, Lord, were he only a great centipede
I might get my fill of the viewing, indeed,
Of Jamie T. Denovan's legs."

And so we beseech you, dear Jamie, fine fellow,
Exhibit what turns this poor maiden to Jell-O—
More fair than the limbs of Annette Funicello—
Those Jamie T. Denovan legs.

Hibernian Holiday

On Saint Patrick's Day we gathered for a typical Hibernian celebration: drinking John Jamison's whiskey, dancing to the tune of fiddle and harp, and singing the auld songs such as, "Does Yer Mother Know You're Irish?"

Cities on the Sound

She's called The Emerald City
and she rises from the bay,
Sittin' with her "pinkie" crooked
while sippin' Chardonnay;
The place that's named Seattle stands,
superior and aloof,
Looking down on other towns—
she thinks them quite uncouth.

The gem of the Pacific Coast,
The Queen of Puget Sound,
She looks with haughty, frosty stare
at everyone around;
A paragon of culture, well,
at least in her own view,
Her citizens cerebral are;
her blood is royal blue.

Now, down The Sound, Tacoma stands,
some thirty miles away,
A working town, its sleeves rolled up,
exerting night and day;
Its docks, its mills, its tide-flat plants
befoul the air down here—
Aroma of Tacoma is
the Emerald City sneer.

But, yet, I guess that I prefer
an honest working town
That's plain and unpretentious,
and where working stiffs abound;
With calloused hands and sweating brows,
they do what must be done—
The difficult and dirty jobs
that really are no fun.

And, found nearby, are Bremerton,
Fort Lewis, and McCord,
Where freedom's guardians reside,
a dedicated horde
Of noble, proud Americans
who serve their country well;
Who'll bravely go where they are asked,
though it's the gates of Hell.

So, though I think Seattle's fine,
and wouldn't run it down,
I'd have to say, on further thought,
it's not my kind of town.
And, if I had to make a choice,
I guess I'm not alone,
I'd have to pick Tacoma—
it just fits my "comfort zone".

Spam

A couple of years ago I received, as a Christmas gift, a little book titled *Spamku*, a collection of haiku-style verses addressing various aspects of the subject canned meat. Inspired to try my own hand at this genre, I turned out this pair. Those who recall our troop's views of Spam will recognize that the first of the pair is pretty tongue-in-cheek. The other suggests a new, and novel, use for the product.

Hordes of ex-G.I.s,
Veterans of World War Two,
Sing thy praise, oh, Spam.

Spam inside my shoes
Softens every jogging step—
Fried, it makes good soles.

Reelin' Robins

Beneath an old crab apple tree
In springtime I have found
The little fruits of last year's crop
Are littering the ground
For, falling downward to the lawn
Because their lives are spent,
I see them scattered all about—
They lie there and ferment.

At times I spot a robin flock
Assembled 'neath the tree;
They're pecking the forbidden fruit,
Then furthermore I'll see
Them lurch about, they weave a bit,
And hiccup now and then—
It seems they never in their lives
Have learned the word is "when."

I move toward the gathering,
Then one big surly guy
Presents me with a wicked scowl
And quite a jaundiced eye—
I back away, concede the ground;
Who ever would have thunk
I'd have to face a robin who's
Belligerent when drunk?

So, spring is sprung, and life is fun,
And robins have a ball

When sugar in the apple juice
Converts to alcohol.
Yet, with the morn comes punishment—
They'll rise up from their beds,
And search for little bags of ice
To place upon their heads.

Yet, now we do our best to help,
To ease their morning pain,
To clear their tongues and aching heads,
And make them well again;
We find that they're much happier
Because, at last, you see
We're putting Bromo Seltzer
In the feeder 'neath the tree.

Women – Sights to Be Held

Sleeping Beauty, or Timing is Everything

Thoughts on the young lady's first words when she awakened from a hundred-year sleep to see a handsome prince bending over her with puckered lips.

A lovely princess, long ago,
Was put into a sleep—
A witch's spell upon her cast,
To slumber long and deep;
Condemned to lie a hundred years,
Until this snoring miss
Would be awakened at the last
By love's first tender kiss.

A handsome prince, when time had come,
Approached where she was stashed;
Rode many miles, 'till saddle sore,
Then through the thicket slashed.
He nimbly scaled the castle wall;
And to her chamber came,
To rouse her from her lengthy nap—
Prince Charming was his name.

He bent above her lovely face,
Unable to resist,
He puckered up, then overcome,
Her ruby lips he kissed;
She opened up her eyes, and smiled,
Then whispered in his ear,
"I'm glad you came; but not tonight—
I've got a headache, dear."

My Darlin's in the Public Domain

I once had a discussion regarding the fact that three different country-western songs had identical melodies. One possibility considered was that all three used an old melody brought over from the British Isles, a not uncommon practice, and that the copyright, if any, had expired. This brought the thought that a copyright running out might have more than one application, so, dipping into the style of Appalachia, the following is offered; a tale of a rake hoist by his own petard.

Now I'm sittin' all alone
With her whereabouts unknown,
While somebody else is playin' my refrain
And there isn't any doubt
That my copyright's run out,
And my darlin's in the public domain.

She was just a simple thing
When I met her in the spring,
An unmarked page on which to write my song;
As the summer passed I wrote
Out the lyrics and the notes—
I could see that I was bringin' her along.

She was very quick to learn,
And I watched the lady turn
From a sweet and shy and backward country maid
To a playful painted doll
Who soon found the way that all
The sophisticated city games were played.

When I met this simple miss,
Why, she couldn't hardly kiss;
When we started out she wasn't worth a darn.
But she learned to drink and smoke
And to tell off-color jokes,
And some other things I taught her in the barn.

The romantic tune I'd planned
Started gettin' out of hand
As she widened out her circle of pursuits,
And I noticed by-and-by
That she had a rovin' eye
For those fellers in five-hundred-dollar boots.

Soon she'd tied me up in knots,
As she toured the singles spots;
My arrangement wasn't one to hold her long;
Now my lonely nights are spent
Wond'rin' where the hell she went,
And what other guy is playin' her my song.

Yes, I'm sittin' all alone
With her whereabouts unknown,
While somebody else is playin' my refrain,
And there isn't any doubt
That my copyright's run out,
And my darlin's in the public domain.

Marriage Incentives, or Mother Knows Best

(Based upon advice one of my classmates always received when she was leaving for a date.)

Oft times a young girl's need to wed
Depends a lot on whether
She's heeded mom's admonishment
To keep her knees together.

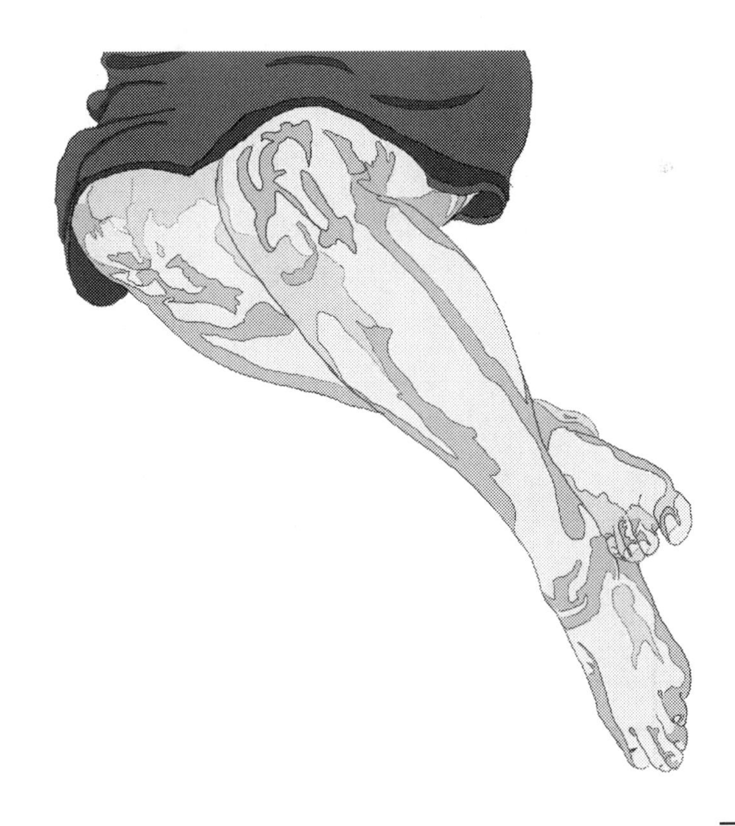

The Girls of Carbon County

Rambling thoughts on the days of my youth.

Some fellows pine for movie stars
Who grace the silver screen;
Some dream of fashion models
With their limbs so long and lean;
Yet, when it comes to seeking mates
Well, if the truth be known,
The French say "chacun à son goût,"
That is, to each his own.

Now, in my youthful search for love
My plan was not so grand,
I fixed my sights primarily
On those most close at hand;
My choice dictated heavily
By mere propinquity—
The girls of Carbon County
Were quite good enough for me.

Now, that is not in any way
To denigrate these girls
They had their charms, and features from
Far places of the world;
Their parents came from many lands,
Wherever coal was mined,
And settled in our county for
The jobs that they could find.

And so, what pleased a young man's eye
In many foreign lands
Was also often to be found
In these girls, close at hand;
The charms of Scandinavia,
The Balkans, Greece, and Spain,
Of Italy, Japan, and Wales
From beautiful to plain.

And so I wasn't too deprived
By choosing from this lot.
I looked them over carefully
And liked the one I got;
We've been together sixty years,
So you can clearly see
My girl from Carbon County—
More than good enough for me.

Chests

A buxom young miss from Beirut,
When told that her chest was a "beaut,"
Replied, "For a sweater
I've not seen one better—
It's cedar, and moth-proof to boot."

Barb, the Babe from Bickleton

My friend Barbara hales from the small farming community of Bickleton, Washington. Bickleton's main claim to fame is the myriad birdhouses the locals have set up for the bluebirds that flock there each spring to nest and raise their families. A distinction of lesser note is the limited gene pool among the human population.

'Twas, let's say, several years ago,
For what the info's worth,
That Barb, the babe from Bickleton
Appeared upon this earth.
A farmer's daughter through and through,
Red cheeked, wide eyed, corn fed,
Barefooted, playing in the fields,
With hayseeds on her head.

As time went by and Barbara grew
Into a lissome miss
She wondered who would be the boy
To first bestow a kiss.
And though the lads were plentiful—
I mean, about a dozen—
The only problem was that Barb
To each one was a cousin.

So, when time came to find a mate
Barb had to leave the scene;
It seemed like she and local lads
Shared far too many genes;
And so, to marry one of them
Would be extremely dumb—
Their kids would likely have three eyes
And six or seven thumbs.

One spring, when bluebird chicks had fledged,
Abandoning their nests,
Young Barbara, too, abandoned hers
Considering it best
To search about, and look for what
The wider world might yield—
At worst, she'd likely have the chance
To go and play the field.

So, Barb set out and scanned the men
For someone who would do;
And she had opportunities,
I'd guess more than a few.
She looked about and chanced upon
A most enticing guy—
Young Rowdy Ron from Richland was
The one that took her eye.

Now, Rowdy Ron, a roguish lad,
Espied her bye and bye,
And Barb, the babe from Bickleton
Becalmed his roving eye;
And though, thus far, he had enjoyed
The fickle, flirting game
'Twas Barb, the babe from Bickleton
Who set his heart aflame.

And so the two connected and
At last became a pair;
They've been together happy years,
And life is sweet and fair.
Together down life's primrose path
They're strolling hand in hand,
Fair Barb, the babe from Bickleton,
And Rowdy Ron, her man.

Skierette

Here is a fetching winter scene, dedicated to Janet, who prefers downhill to cross-country.

Behold the perky skierette,
In powder to her knees,
Skirting cliffs and leaping brush
And skimming through the trees.
She runs the frigid, snowy slopes,
A grin upon her face,
With frosted tresses out behind
And dimples froze in place.

Poems I Wouldn't Show My Kid Sister

This poem addresses the fact that kid sisters are not necessarily as naïve as overprotective big brothers might sometimes believe and hope. It presents an imagined encounter between me and the kid sister that I might have had.

I bought a little book of poems
  and took it home today;
Then, poring o'er a page or two,
  I found it quite risqué.
I further scanned, then came the thought,
  "Good golly, holy gee,
This book contains a lot of stuff
  kid sister shouldn't see."

Alas, I had to rush away—
  an urgent errand burned—
But hid the book, quite safe, I thought,
  until I had returned.
Arriving back, at last inside,
  I saw to my surprise,
Kid sister leafing through the book
  with bright and shining eyes.

Right quick I grabbed it from her hand
  and cried, "You mustn't look!
Some words quite unfamiliar

are found within this book;
And if you read it, dear, I fear,
and see such words as these,
'Twill bring a blush, and too, offend
your sensibilities."

She gently drew me to her side
and softly squeezed my hand,
Then said, "Just whisper in my ear
those you don't understand."
She smiled, "Girls aren't as innocent
as brothers might suppose,
And I've heard many times before
words cruder far than those.

Let's read this book together now;
we'll scan it line by line
I'll teach you 'till your knowledge, dear,
is just as great as mine."

Song of an Amateur Beautician

When my daughter dropped over for a visit recently we complimented her on her appearance. She remarked that she had just got her eyebrows waxed, which led to the following train of thought.

The time had come around again
to get my eyebrows waxed,
Yet when I checked my credit card
I found that it was "maxed,"
And since I didn't have the cash
for my beautician's fee
I figured if I got 'em waxed
the job was up to me.

I searched my home, but paraffin
was nowhere to be found.
"Well, wax is wax," I told myself,
and further looked around.
To find a worthy substitute,
I hunted high and low,
Then looked beneath the sink and found
a pint of Mop & Glo.

It didn't list "Ingredients"
to tell if wax was one,

But I applied a bit of thought
then told myself, "Well, Hon,
It says it gives your floor a gloss,
so think about the facts—
If it will make your flooring glow,
it has to have some wax."

I carefully applied the stuff
upon my hairy brow;
I spread it on, then rubbed and buffed—
American know-how—
For when the job was finished, well,
it seems it turned out fine,
The eyebrows hadn't thinned a bit—
but, lordy, how they shine.

Jean

A charming sight near the outlet of Lake Wenatchee.

What a pretty scene;
Jean;
Auburn hair agleam
On a log beside a stream;
Makes a fellow dream—
Dream
—Of Jean.

Kelly, the Rail Splittin' Wife

A friend of mine and her husband have turned their back yard into a garden, growing both flowers and vegetables. They also have four chickens and a rabbit. One day she told me that she had spent the morning splitting firewood. Somehow out of all this grew the following picture:

Sequestered far down in a valley,
Away from the wild city strife,
A farmer attends his green acres
With Kelly, his partner and wife.
They've chosen a setting most rustic
To live out the days of their lives;
Their holdings appear reminiscent
Of etchings by Currier and Ives.

Their labors defined by this couple—
He works with the mule and the plow
At tilling the crops and the garden,
And Kelly draws milk from the cow.
He's tasked to provide for the livestock,
Their feeding and all of the rest,
While Kelly strews grain for the chickens,
Then cheerfully plunders their nests.

Yet, with this division of labor,
They have certain tasks they must share;
With mattocks and shovels and axes
They pitch in to do what is fair;
And jobs that require sweat and muscle
Are jointly performed by the two;
Hard tasks such as building the fences
Involve work they both have to do.

While Farmer is plying the augur,
And working out fencing details,
His Kelly, way off in the wood lot,
Is splitting the logs into rails.
Equipped with her maul and her wedges
She gives it the best that she can,
And, much as John Henry's gal, Polly,
Fair Kelly drives steel like a man.

So Kelly conjures up an image
That borders a bit on the weird,
She puts one in mind of Abe Lincoln—
Excepting, of course, for the beard.
Yet, Farmer is fully contented
To live out the days of his life
Attending his forty-plus acres
With Kelly, his rail-splittin' wife.

Philosophy and Other Foolishness

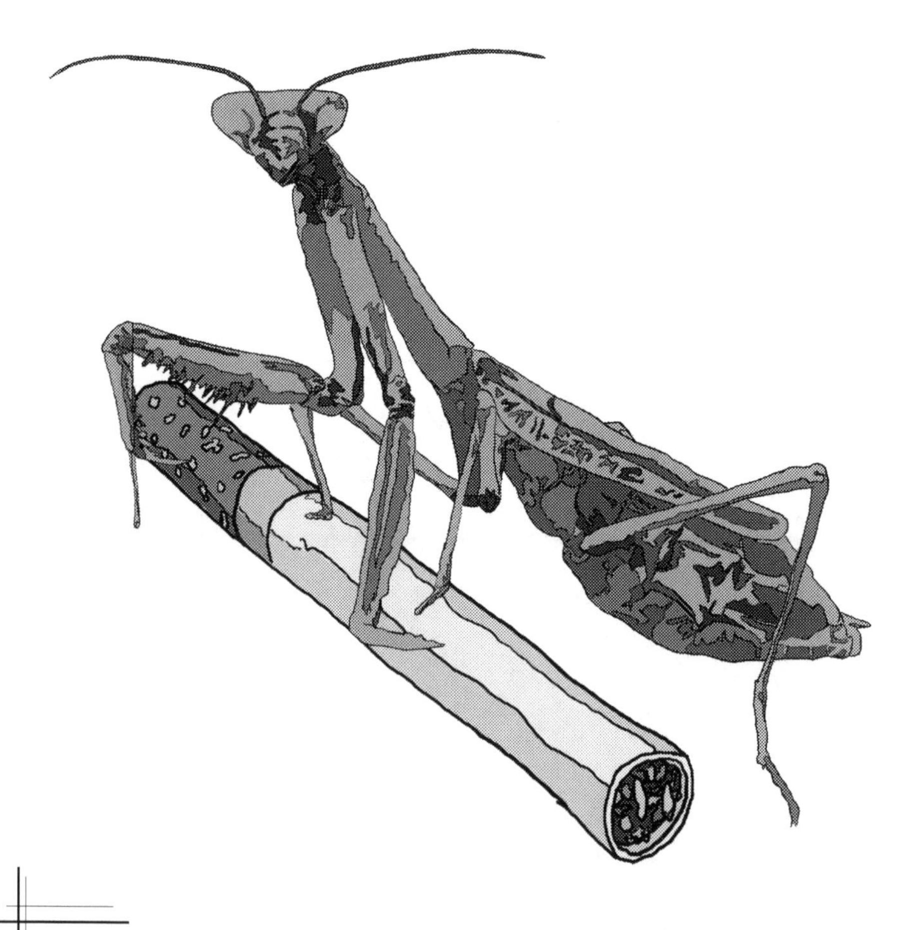

Aftermaths

(Thoughts on the love life of the praying mantis.)

I've heard, with praying mantises,
Whene'er they chance to mate,
The groom is treated by his bride
To quite a dismal fate—
For when the act's completed, well,
This may appear unreal,
She turns around and slaughters him,
And has him for a meal.

Now this would seem sheer cruelty
And quite beyond the pale,
The way the lady winds it up
By dining on the male,
Yet it's not animosity
That makes her act this way;
I guess it's merely what is known
As mantis after play.

But there may be an upside here:
Their kids come out on top;
They never have to purchase gifts
To give to dear old Pop,
For Father's Day is meaningless
To this half-orphaned band
Of children who've resulted from
Their parents' one-night stand.

And, yet, for mantis' aftermath
'Twould better seem by far
To have the mating pair refrain
From post-coital war;
He'd live a long and happy life
And come off better yet
If she would just relax, lean back,
And have a cigarette.

Now, human folk are different,
And when love making's done,
Guys find a nicer follow up
As encore to their fun:
Their lady's apt to warm them with
A snuggle and a hug—
So thank your stars that you were born
A human, not a bug.

Orville Redenbacher's Popcorn and Erlanger Beer

Some years ago a new, and purportedly superior, brewery product called Erlanger Beer appeared on the market. At that time a popcorn, Orville Redenbacher's, was also being advertised as a superior product. This brought forth the following thought regarding food and drink for the elite among the Country Folks. After a fairly short time, Erlanger Beer disappeared from our local scene. Let this poem serve as the memorial for this deceased brew.

I've heard it said that everyone
        acquires his special tastes;
Raw oysters, snails, or haggis,
        even gander-liver pastes.
I've tried 'em all and yet I find
        my choice is very clear:
Orville Redenbacher's popcorn and Erlanger beer.

Now, city folks drink fine champagne
        a-bubblin' in the glass,
And caviar for munchies

is their notion of true class,
But out here in the country,
you will find that we revere
Orville Redenbacher's popcorn and Erlanger Beer.

For everyday consumption
almost anything will do,
A pocket full of pork rinds
and a glass of three-point-two.
But fancier occasions move us
to a higher tier—
Orville Redenbacher's popcorn and Erlanger Beer.

Confronted by a manager
who didn't like my style,
I buttered up his steno,
who responded with a smile
And slipped to me the secret
of advancing my career:
Give him Redenbacher's popcorn and Erlanger Beer.

I sat down by a "nine-point-five"
one evening in a bar,
And wondered to myself what might
entice her to my car;
She must have read my mind, because
she whispered in my ear,
"Buy me Redenbacher's popcorn and Erlanger Beer."

I had a dream the other night:
my life had reached its end;
I stumbled to the Pearly Gates,
my record to defend.
Saint Peter smiled and said, "Come in,
I'm sure you'll like it here,
We serve Redenbacher's popcorn and Erlanger Beer."

So, if you find you're feeling low
    and life has lost its zest,
Just take a lesson from my book;
    feel free, come be my guest;
And switch to what will banish
    every frown and sigh and tear—
Orville Redenbacher's popcorn and Erlanger Beer.

Retirement

(Based upon the expressed concerns of my wife's friends that I would be constantly underfoot and interfering when I retired.)

It seemed like ages that I'd toiled
to pay for food and rent
Until at last I reached my goal—
I'd earned retirement.
No more the dreaded nine-to-five,
no days of sweat and strife,
I'd gained the opportunity
to live the leisure life.

So now I've reached the golden years
and life is fair and sweet;
I'm kicked back in my easy chair,
a Shih-Tzu at my feet.
Now, propped before my TV set
and thumbing the remote,
I've found the only way to live—
at least, that gets my vote.

I call out to the kitchen
in a voice that's loud and clear,
"Hey, Babe, my glass is empty—
would you bring another beer?
And, Honey, while you're doing so

and come to fetch my brew,
I need a snack, so bring along
some chips and salsa, too."

Yet life's not total idleness;
I have my simple chores:
Observing and critiquing as
she dusts and sweeps the floors,
Providing frequent guidance
such as, "Dear, you missed that spot."
I mean it to be useful,
and I'm sure it helps a lot.

And when the wife has visitors
I don't just sit and yawn,
But now and then participate
in what is going on.
Yet I don't try to dominate,
just say, now and again,
"Hey, ladies, would you hold it down
so I can hear John Wayne?"

Ah, yes, retirement's heavenly,
I find this life is great,
And daily I reflect on this
and so inform my mate;
Yet her response is odd to me—
it seems quite strange, but true—
Regarding my retirement,
she has another view.

So while I'm well intentioned
and I try to do my best,
I find it rather puzzling
and fear I must confess

My wife has quite a problem.
I don't understand it, but
She seems to think that I've become
a pain in "you know what."

On Aging

I've pondered o'er the years I've lived
and found myself confused,
The name bestowed by Mom and Dad
was hardly ever used;
And so I had to recognize
'twas me that folks addressed.
They used no term unique to me,
distinguished from the rest.

I harken to the long ago
when I was just a lad,
The bloom of youth upon my cheeks—
back then, the names I had—
The ones I learned to answer to
when all was said and done,
Were "Honey" from the ladies, and
the men all called me "Son."

As years elapsed and I matured
I noticed, by and by
Folks looked at me quite differently,
and I was just, "Hey, guy."
All used that terminology
whene'er I was addressed;
They treated me quite casually
as just one of the rest.

Then more years passed, and suddenly,
to my complete surprise,
To ladies, all, I now was “Sir,”
and “Mister” to the guys;
And, now I’ve reached that final stage
until the aging stops;
To guys I’m now “Old Timer,” and
the women call me “Pops.”

Reflections on the Afterlife

I've thought about the afterlife
        and pictured in my mind
When I have left my Earthly home
        the kind of place I'd find;
I visualized soft fields of green
        with hordes of souls arrayed,
Assembled, all, with harp in hand,
        platonic love displayed.

And yet, I thought there must be more;
        it seemed too awful bland
To have to spend eternity
        in such a boring land;
I hoped I'd find an earthly touch
        to set a lighter mood—
If carnal love were not allowed,
        at least there might be food.

I pictured nightly banquets then
        where tasty foods abound,
Where meats and treats, desserts and sweets
        were heaped up all around;
Rich foods, laced with cholesterol
        yet, as the pleasures mount,
Your arteries will never plug,
        and calories won't count.

However, thinking further on,
these lovely, sumptuous feeds
Bring other factors into play,
like sanitation needs.
I'd guess there'd be facilities
with toilets there, as well,
That empty most directly to
the kitchens down in Hell.

And so, my friends, behave yourselves
in this, your earthly life;
Don't risk your soul by doing wrong;
avoid crime, sin, and strife;
Or 'stead of eating Heaven's food
up with the angel troop
You'll spend eternity in Hell
ingesting angel poop.

Chocolate

Recent stories in our local newspaper told about a young Chesapeake Bay retriever that had been roaming about the countryside with two badly crippled front legs. A lady had taken the dog in, but hadn't the resources to continue caring for it and was looking for someone to adopt it or provide the needed medical services. The dog, which she had dubbed Chocolate because of its color, had been moving about either by crawling or by walking on its two sound hind legs. The one constant in the dog's life, and apparently its only tie to a happier past, was a squishy, knobby, yellow ball, which it took with it wherever it went. The major news media picked up the story, and offers for contributions, medical aid, and adoption poured in. At first the veterinarians weren't sure whether the dog could be repaired, or would have to be put down. At that point I was moved to write the following poem.

Oh, Chocolate, you wondrous dog,
You roamed the fields alone,
No master to look after you,
Completely on your own;
Your forelegs broken, badly healed,
Could serve you but to crawl;
Your only friend and family,
A squishy yellow ball.

How you survived, as months elapsed,
We can't exactly say;
Did pilfered scraps from nearby farms
Sustain you day-to-day?
Yet you survived, and moved about
By sound hind legs propelled;
Each time you moved, inside your mouth
Your yellow ball was held.

But, then, one day a kindly soul
Observed and spread the word.
Responses were immediate
Among the folks who heard.
Donations came, arrangements made
For vet hospital care,
With offers for adoption
Pouring in from everywhere.

Now you're receiving proper care,
Your shattered limbs to mend,
We wish you well and hope your tale
Achieves a happy end,
With forelegs strong, and love around,
The wishes of us all—
Secure in an adopted home,
You and your yellow ball.

Yet, should the fates rule otherwise,
And if your soul's called home,
Oh, plucky dog, you'll be with God;
You'll lie beside his throne.
"Hey, Chocolate, good boy, go fetch,"
You'll hear Him softly call;
Then He'll bestow a smile on thee—
And throw your yellow ball.

Postlude:

Within days after this poem was written, surgeries were performed successfully on both of the injured legs, Chocolate was undergoing rehabilitation therapy, and he and his yellow ball were awaiting adoption by one of the dozens of applicants.

You Can't Play the Cello in a Skirt

A young friend of mine who plays cello in the local symphony orchestra once remarked that it is difficult to play the cello while wearing a skirt. This gave me fodder for the following poem.

I've known a few musicians,
and I played a bit myself
Until my lack of talent
put my stuff up on the shelf.
Yet, there's one truth I've clearly learned,
I'll try to keep it curt—
And that's the fact that you cannot
play cello in a skirt.

Now if you play viola
or the little violin,
To hold it is no problem—
it is tucked beneath your chin;
But cellists have few options,
so they really cannot win
Because the bloody instrument
is stuck between their shins.

And if you play the double bass
you're in a standing stance;
You've choices, then, of how you dress,
in shorts or skirts or pants;
But when you play the cello,
it is seated you must be;
You have to keep the blasted thing
tucked in between your knees.

A cellist in a full-length skirt?
pleats foul in strings or bow;
But if you shorten up the skirt,
well, this you need to know:
Your cello must remain in place,
positioned carefully,
Or else you'll find your audience
has much too much to see.

And, if it's the electric kind
remember other stuff;
Their shape and size is different—
they don't conceal enough.
So place them quite strategically
and keep them there with care,
Or else you'll find that you display
your lacy underwear.

And, yet this problem of attire
is mostly gender stuff;
For P. Casals and Yo Yo Ma
decisions aren't so tough.
They're free to dress as e'er they will,
and folks won't really care;
This problem's largely feminine,
although that isn't fair.

Yet, it's not only gender based,
    but tied to culture too,
For kilted Scots the bagpipes play,
    and cellos they eschew
For fear their audience may learn—
    much to their shame and guilt—
The answer to the question, "Lad,
    what's worn beneath the kilt?"

So, when you pick the instrument
    that you would like to play,
Just keep these little thoughts in mind;
    consider, as you may:
Before you pick the cello, dear,
    it really doesn't hurt
To know you cannot play the thing
    and also wear a skirt.

French Horns

As one who admires fine musicians,
I think such performers are swell,
Yet French hornists damage the image,
Their fingers shoved into the bell,
Diverting my mind from the music
To future appointments, for damn,
They serve as a constant reminder
Of upcoming prostate exams.

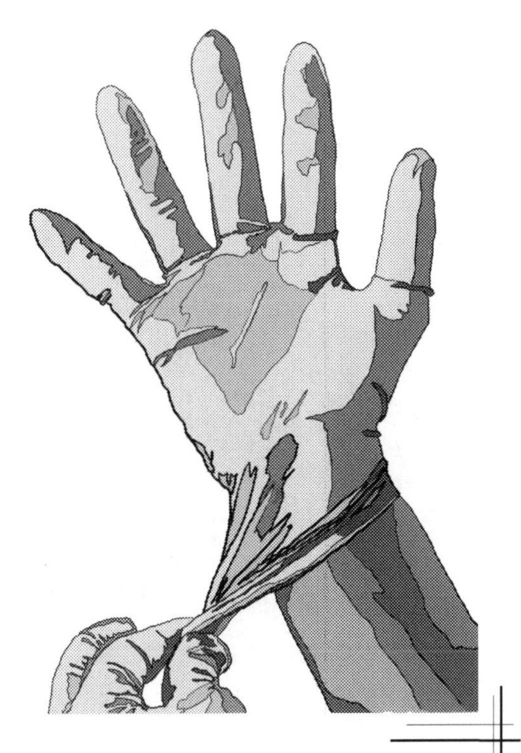

Traffic Trials

At times, in a tangle of traffic,
I get this peculiar sensation;
It's not what I'd really think of as "rage,"
It's more like, well, "road irritation."
The drivers around have no manners;
Their brain cells were checked at The Mall.
I gaze all directions with caution
While cringing in fear of them all.

The lane changing cut-in-and-outers,
The ones who won't move on the green,
The won't-yields, with cell phone addiction,
Can summon up thoughts near obscene.
And yet, I curtail my emotions,
Try not to give in to my ire,
For there are some terms to describe them
Quite proper for use by a choir.

Yet, when my refined remonstrations,
Like, "Watch it, you dork," leave my lips,
I have to beware what I'm saying,
Not wanting inaccurate quips;
For "dork," as you know, is a man's term—
The feminine equal is "ditz,"
And I like to speak with precision,
To use the expression that fits.

So, seeking to speak quite correctly,
The gender I try to discern,
Before I deliver my comments
Intended to make their ears burn.
Obscured by their dark-tinted windows,
It isn't too easy to do,
And if you are able to see them,
Hair length's an inadequate clue.

Now, often, despite my intentions
I still can't discern guy or gal,
And just know, from my observations,
Their driving is terribly foul.
So when I'm completely unable
To know, "Is it dork, is it ditz?"
I just have to use the generic, "dumb (blank)—
(If ladies are present, that's "twits.")

Handles

There's many kinds of handles,
you will find them everywhere;
They're placed upon your pots and pans
and other kitchenware.
Then, when you take yourself outside,
you'll find that, as a rule,
They're stuck onto your shovels
and your other garden tools.

Then, too, there is one's "handle,"
that's the name to one applied,
And also how you're "handling"
the many things you've tried.
Though I've encountered lots of types
while passing through this life,
I've found these my clear favorites—
love handles on my wife.

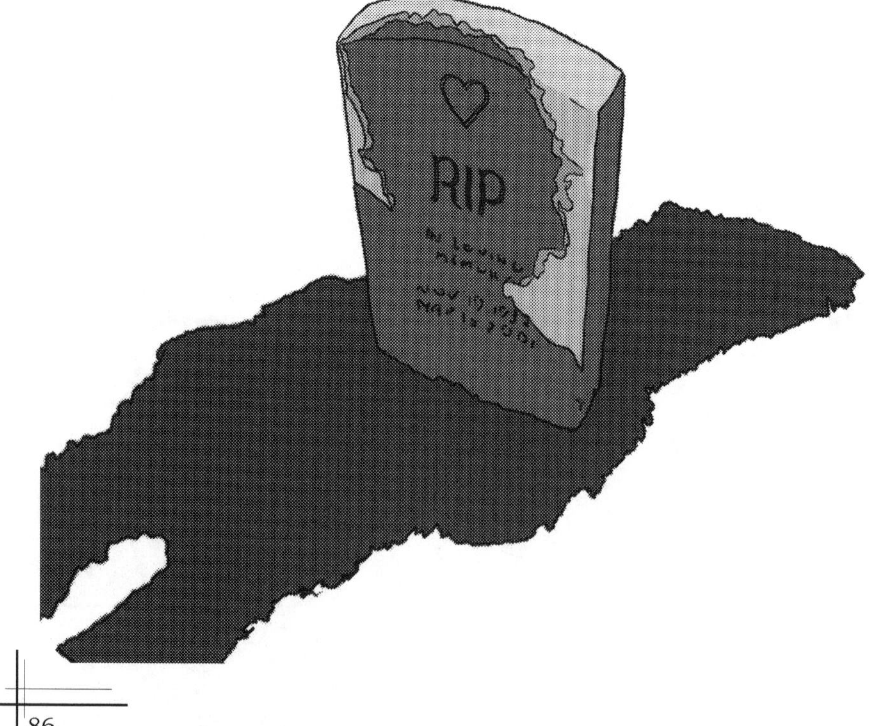
RIP

Epitaph

My cardiac physician once
imparted this advice:
"To live a long and healthy life,
eat lots of beans and rice.
And if it is longevity
that you sincerely wish,
Eat mainly veggies, and for meats,
just chicken breasts and fish."

Well, given my heredity,
I thought it worth a try,
For I felt no great urgency
to lay me down and die.
So I agreed to go along,
decided that I'd opt
My doctor's recommended bland
heart diet to adopt.

Now after years of dining thus,
the meals had lost their charm;
I longed for food that tasted good,
no matter what the harm.
And when it came to chicken breasts,
confirmed what I had heard:
No matter how you flavor it,
that bird still tastes like bird.

I found my dreams were haunted by
the thought of shepherd's pies,
Of Big Mac stacks, washed down by malts,

accompanied by fries,
With bacon, steaks and eggs, all filled
with saturated fat
Then I recalled the basic truth—
that's where the flavor's at.

And so, at last, I told myself,
when all is said and done,
Go for the *quality* of life—
it ought to be some fun.
So why not have, from time to time,
a very tasty meal,
And let the chips fall where they may
and arteries congeal.

I pondered all the pros and cons,
then said, "Oh, what the hell."
Temptation soon had mastered me,
and I was eating well.
So now I lie beneath the sod,
yet you can spare your grief,
For here I sleep contentedly,
my belly full of beef.

Ode to a Surge Protector

A while back my surge protector saved my computer from destruction by a power surge at the cost of its own life. I thought this selfless deed deserved some recognition.

Courageous surge protector,
You answered duty's call;
Protecting my computer parts,
You bravely gave your all.
Your little body intervened
Before my PC tower,
To save it from destruction by
A sudden surge in power.

So now my desktop's still alive
Because of how you're wired;
You did your job, protecting it—
You beeped, and then expired.
And so you have my gratitude—
Take this salute from me:
Courageous surge protector,
I will bid you R. I. P.

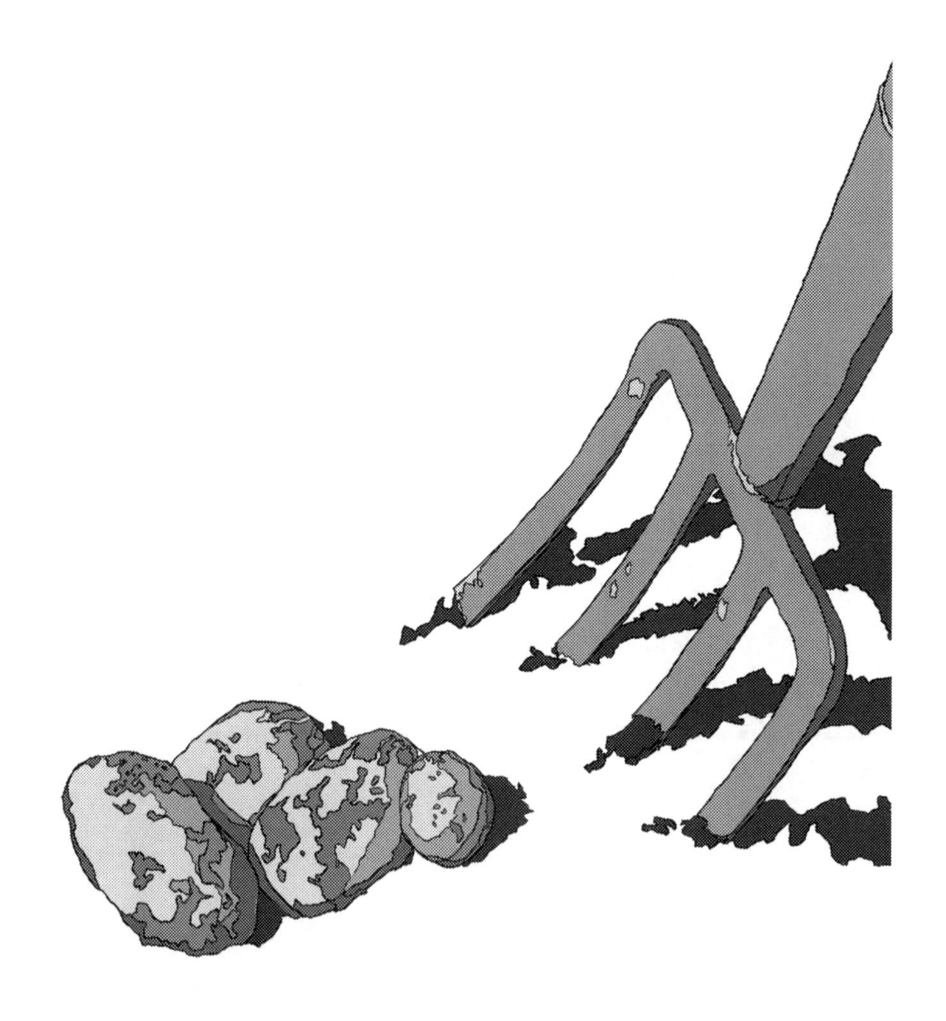

They Don't Eat Grits in Idaho

I recently went into a Denny's restaurant in southeastern Washington and selected the "Two-Egg Breakfast," described as "Two eggs, toast of your choice, and choice of hash browns or grits." The waitress who took my order asked how I would like my eggs cooked and what kind of toast I would like, but didn't ask if I would like grits or hash browns, which led me to believe that grits weren't really an option. Eastern Washington, and the adjoining Idaho areas, are purely potato country. This generated the following thoughts:

It's clearly known that folks who live
  throughout the Sunny South
Delight in stuffing daily bowls
  of grits into their mouth;
But you may find in other states
  that grits are simply duds—
They don't eat grits in Idaho,
  for that's the land of spuds.

You'll find that Idahoans all
  stuff taters in their jaw,
Consuming them in multitudes—
  I think that there's a law

Requiring folks within the state
a quota to fulfill
So Idaho won't disappear
beneath a tater hill.

Yet you can have variety—
this diet isn't bland;
Just use imagination, folks,
so, come on, try your hand,
For you can put them in a soup,
or serve them baked or mashed,
Or you can serve them boiled or fried,
or try them "Frenched" or hashed.

In salads, pancakes, they are found,
and as a doughnut base,
There's even tater "ice cream"
you can stuff into your face.
With multitudes of recipes,
you never need be bored;
You'll find that they are tasty, and
they're wholesome, thank the Lord.

So, loyal Idahoans try
to do their level best
To chew away the tater crop—
I think they'll pass the test.
Though grits are scarffed throughout the land
of chiggers, sweat, and floods,
They don't eat grits in Idaho,
for that's the land of spuds.

Depilation

When I recently started a program of radiation treatments for cancer therapy and was about to begin chemotherapy, I discussed the subject with a friend who has had similar treatments to see what to expect. At the end of our discussion, he said that the experience would probably give me fodder for another poem. Ergo:

I went to see my medico—
I'd had a bit of pain—
He said, "Your chest malignancy
I fear is back again."
We called in my oncologist,
Ran tests which then confirmed
The problems that I'd had before
Had once again returned.

We first considered surgery—
That's what we'd done before—
A pity that we had not then
Installed a swinging door.
We sat and talked of what to do—
What seemed the best for me
Was radiation zaps combined
With chemotherapy.

We spoke of all the pros and cons
Attendant to such care,
Concluded the worst negative
Was merely loss of hair;
Well, I was rather far along
To balding of my pate,
So thought the loss of what remained
Was not a tragic fate.

Then, too, I thought my mustache loss,
If it should go away,
Was something I could rectify
With upper lip toupee.
My daughter had her tresses trimmed
And handed me a lock;
We tied it up and glued it on,
Then had a bit of shock.

I was no more my dapper self,
No movie star was I;
I didn't look like Errol Flynn,
No David Niven guy.
The image that I first beheld
Showed me 'twas all too true:
I was no Douglas Fairbanks, but
Much more like Fu Manchu.

And other spots had lost their hair—
It left me quite surprised
To find my alopecia
Was far from localized.
For now that winter's coming on,
Well, if the truth be told,
I'm finding out that both my head
And private parts get cold.

So, here in my declining years
I've lost a bit of charm,
Resulting from the treatments that
Keep me from further harm;
I've taken lumps, but as I now
Reflect on what's ahead—
I ain't the man I used to be,
But, dammit, I ain't dead.

Love on the Internet

(Based on spam I sometimes receive on my internet messenger service.)

I glanced at my computer screen
and there I chanced to see
A message: gals were dying
to engage in sex with me.
I'm not quite sure about these folks,
or what they think is fun;
I have my faults, but dammit,
necrophilia isn't one.

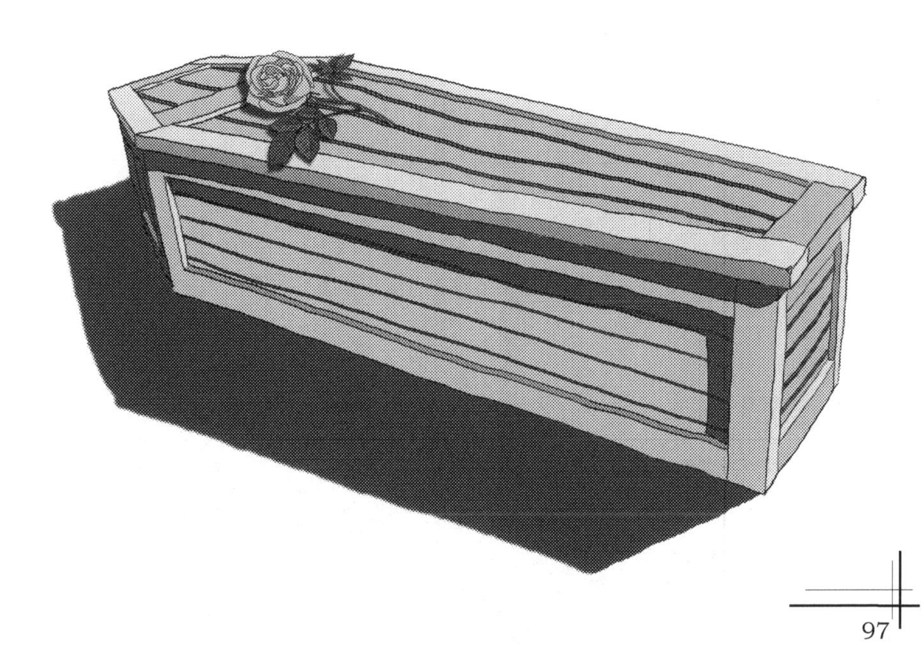

Canine Contemplations

One day in the city park I noticed a Saint Bernard and a Shih Tzu in close proximity, which generated the following thoughts. I changed the dog's breeds to make the poem flow properly, but the thought is the same. For those who may not know, a papillon is a little lap dog. A mastiff, of course, is at the other end of the canine size spectrum.

The lessons of philosophy
One finds most anywhere;
Example: walking through the park
To get a bit of air,
I spied a horde of canine folk
Of every breed and size,
Some eying others warily,
Some sniffing butts and thighs.

Among the sights that filled my eye
From my detached position,
What seemed to me exemplary
Of ultimate ambition,
'Twas 'bout as close to "In your dreams,"
As one is apt to find:
A mastiff, and a papillon
With romance on his mind.

But then, I thought, a lesson's here;
There's something to be learned.
I mulled it over in my mind,
And to this fact it turned:
Though you may have your handicaps,
It really doesn't matter—
To climb and reach your lofty goals,
You might just need a ladder.

The Gang

In my youth I was part of a tightly knit group of young fellows who gathered regularly to have a good time. We and our friends and families referred to us as "The Gang," although we were in no way gangsters or thugs. After recently hearing of the passing of two more members of the group, I was moved to look back and write this poem of commemoration. I thought it a fitting poem to close out this book.

The year was nineteen forty-six,
We'd ended World War Two,
With servicemen returning home,
Their futures to pursue;
A group of us, in Helper Town
Each evening would collect
To court the girls, to drink some brew,
And raise a little heck.

Though most of us were veterans,
There were another few
Who hadn't yet put in their time
But joined in with the crew;
We knew them from our high school days,
We felt that they belonged,
So opened up our membership
To add them to the throng.

The membership was fluid,
From a dozen to a score,
Yet twelve or so solidified
To form the basic core
Of Jay and Boofo, Al and Clyde,
Of Max and Mouse and Fenn,
Of Cheesie, Guy, Kennuck (that's me),
And Hollie, Sacco, Ken.

Then time went by, and we dispersed
To weddings, jobs, and school;
Though parted geographically,
We felt it would be cool
To keep in touch, meet when we could,
As best as we could do—
We stuck together through the years—
And Hollie was the glue.

As more years passed, we dropped away
By one and one and one,
Until we're just the remnants now—
Our Gang is nearly done.
We're whittled down to just a few,
Our numbers only three;
The last survivors, Cheesie, Clyde
And, yes, Kennuck—that's me.

Yet we survivors, hanging on,
Our years four score and more,
Anticipate what lies ahead,
What fate's reserved in store;
So not too many years from now
We'll gather by and by
And join with the departed in
Some tavern in the sky.